Black Wolf of the Glacier

Alaska's Romeo

by Deb Vanasse

illustrated by Nancy Slagle

University of Alaska Press
P.O. Box 756240
Fairbanks, AK 99775-6240

ISBN 978-1-60223-197-9

Library of Congress Cataloging-in-Publication Data

Vanasse, Deb.
Black wolf of the glacier : Alaska's Romeo / by Deb Vanasse.
pages cm
Summary: When a lonely wolf makes friends with her dog, Shawna's fear turns
to love. Based on the true story of Romeo, a wolf who lived near Juneau's
Mendenhall Glacier and lost his wolfpack as a young male.
ISBN 978-1-60223-197-9 (pbk. : alk. paper)
1. Wolves—Alaska—Juvenile fiction. [1. Wolves—Fiction.
2. Human-animal relationships—Fiction. 3. Alaska—Fiction.] I. Title.
PZ10.3.V254Bl 2013
[E]—dc23

2012032609

Cover and text layout by Paula Elmes

This publication was printed on acid-free paper that meets the minimum requirements for
ANSI / NISO Z39.48–1992 (R2002) (Permanence of Paper for Printed Library Materials)

Printed in China

Long and low, a howl pierced the night.

In warm houses near the frozen lake, dogs perked their ears. Shawna hugged Buddy's neck as he whined at the window. "What's wrong?" she asked.

Again the wolf howled. Inside the house, Buddy barked. Ruff! Ruff! "It's all right," Shawna whispered. "I'm here."

His cries met only with silence, the wolf curled in the snow. His breath frosted his thick, black fur as he slept alone in a sliver of moonlight.

When dawn flooded the sky, the wolf stretched in front of a blue-streaked glacier.

He cocked his head at a rustle from under the snow.

With his big front paws he pounced and pounced until at last he caught a small vole.

After his meager breakfast, the wolf warmed himself in the sun on a big rock, an erratic left by the glacier. He waited and watched. Maybe this was the day another wolf would appear. A playmate. A friend. Or maybe a whole pack of wolves, like the one he'd roamed with when he was a pup.

When the sun dipped in a low arc toward the mountains, the black wolf slipped into the woods. From the trail came the *swoosh, swoosh* of skis in the snow.

Ears erect, he froze at a flash of bright red and the
swishing tail of a dog. From his hidden place in the
trees, the wolf whined.

Buddy stopped. He sniffed the cold air, then growled from deep in his throat.

Swoosh, swoosh. "Come on," called Shawna.
Buddy bounded after her. The wolf watched
as they disappeared in the forest.

The next day when the sun slid toward the mountains, the wolf padded through the snow to the trail. When he heard the *swoosh* of skis and saw the flash of red and the dog's swishing tail, he lifted his nose and howled.

Shawna steadied her hand on
Buddy's back. "Easy," she said.

Buddy ducked from under her hand.
He charged at the wolf. *Ruff! Ruff!
Ruff!* Buddy barked.

The wolf sprang from the trees.

"No!" Shawna cried.

The wolf circled, so close that his frozen breath met Buddy's. He spread his front paws and lowered his head. *Ruff! Ruff!* The wolf barked.

Buddy leapt, whirled, and dashed through the snow. The wolf chased after him.

"Come, Buddy!" Shawna called. "Come now!"

Snow sprayed as Buddy and the wolf dashed in circles. Buddy wagged his tail. The wolf wagged his tail back.

Shawna dropped her hands from her face. Panting, Buddy squared off with the wolf, his eyes bright. *Play with me*, the wolf seemed to say as he pranced in front of the dog. Snow flew, the two chasing each other until both were worn out.

Before long, the wolf made more friends. He followed dogs over trails and across the frozen lake. Like Shawna, people around the lake came to trust and respect him. They let the wolf approach first and stayed back as he played with their dogs. Because he was so loving, someone gave him a name: Romeo.

Wildlife

ROMEO WINS HEARTS AND NOSES

Visitors to the Mendenhall Glacier area near Juneau, Alaska, have seen more and more appearances from the mysterious lone wolf some call Romeo. Visitors with dogs are the most common recipients of Romeo's attentions. All those who encounter Romeo seem to agree that his presence carries a certain grandeur.

"I was a little frightened at first, and so were Pugsy and Lulu," remarked one bystander. "But we quickly realized that all he wanted was a meet-and-greet, and not a power lunch. Very shortly, the three of us were disarmed by his rogueish charm." Romeo has never appeared as part of a pack, so wildlife biologist Dr. Roberts speculates that the wolf hunts on his own. Fortunately, dogs and people of all sizes do not seem to constitute a major part of his diet. Local scientists speculate that he feeds primarily on a diet of small rodents. His den, likely situated somewhere near Mendenhall Glacier, has not been located.

"Romeo's behavior is something of an anomaly," comments Dr. Roberts. "We are seeing more and more such dog-wolf interactions from feral creatures as human activity increasingly infringes upon forest boundaries, but Romeo is still an unusual case." Romeo's errand in departing the forest is still ambiguous, but so far, snacks don't seem to entice him, and he generally steers clear of garbage cans. His interest in people and dogs suggests that his errand is social, but as to exactly what he wants, we're still not entirely certain.

PUFFINS DELIGHT CRUISE TOURISTS

Every year, thousands of tourists flock to Alaskan cruises to experience firsthand the feathered majesty of wild puffins. These noble birds nest on cliffs that limn Alaska's southern coast, especially in areas around Valdez. Puffins are darlings of many cruise ships that traverse the coastal and glacial waters of southern Alaska. Tourists frequently find themselves spellbound by the dignified yet portly shape of these pelagic seabirds. "They resemble penguins, but are much more svelte," remarked one tourist. "I am fascinated by the fact that their wings can lift them off the ice at all." Captains who guide coastal tours assure their passengers that Puffins are not at all carnivorous, and feed primarily on zooplankton. Once a year, they shed and regrow their colorful outer beaks. Tourists be warned: most cruises do not allow puffin hunting.

RAT ISLANDS WILL BE RAT FREE, AUTHORITIES CLAIM

Rat Island, a 10-square-mile land mass amid the similarly named archipelago, has almost shaken free of its rat problem. This volcanic remnant was infested with brown rats by a Japanese shipwreck in 1780. Invasive rats are also present on 16 other islands in the Aleutian chain. The rats are said to pose a significant threat to indigenous seabirds, such as the Aleutian cackling geese, which have no natural defense against the rodents. The US Fish and Wildlife Service is formulating plans to eradicate the rats from the island in the hopes of one day changing the island's name and attracting tourism. One local inhabitant suggested introducing cats, but the Aleutian cackling geese blackballed this idea immediately.

WHEN ALL ELSE FAILS, TIE THIS FLY

The Raincountry Flyfishers will meet at 7 p.m. on Wednesday, Feb. 15 in the Thunder Mountain High School library.

Tony Marsters will instruct participants on how to tie a fly that he said has worked very well for cohos on the Juneau roadside. He calls it the "When All Else Fails" fly, but uses it sparingly.

"It is a little more time consuming to tie than most other coho flies but it can really save the day," Marsters said.

The fly is basically a half-and-half but tied flat-wing style on a sixty-degree jig hook with added features that trigger strikes.

The Raincountry Flyfishers will provide materials for anyone wishing to tie along. A basic fly tying kit will be provided for anyone new to fly tying if requested in advance.

Soon the wolf became famous. Photos of Romeo were sent near and far. He had fans not only at the glacier but all over the world.

Romeo didn't know he was a star. He sprinted and hunted and played like any other wolf. Sometimes he'd brush against Shawna's red coat as he trotted with Buddy, so close she could see the gray streaks in his thick, black fur and the scar on his muzzle.

DO NOT FEED

MENDENHALL LAKE WOLF

Some people worried that a wolf shouldn't play the way Romeo did. Rangers talked about moving him far from the glacier. But Romeo's human friends convinced them to hang signs instead, reminders that even a friendly wild wolf needs his space.

For six years, Romeo lived peacefully near Mendenhall Glacier.

Though he still slept alone, he spent his days romping with friends.

Then one September day when the lake shimmered with the colors of fall and frost nipped the air, the black wolf of the glacier vanished.

Shawna searched the woods. Buddy sniffed the trails. He barked. He scanned the trees. He whined for his friend. But there was no answer.

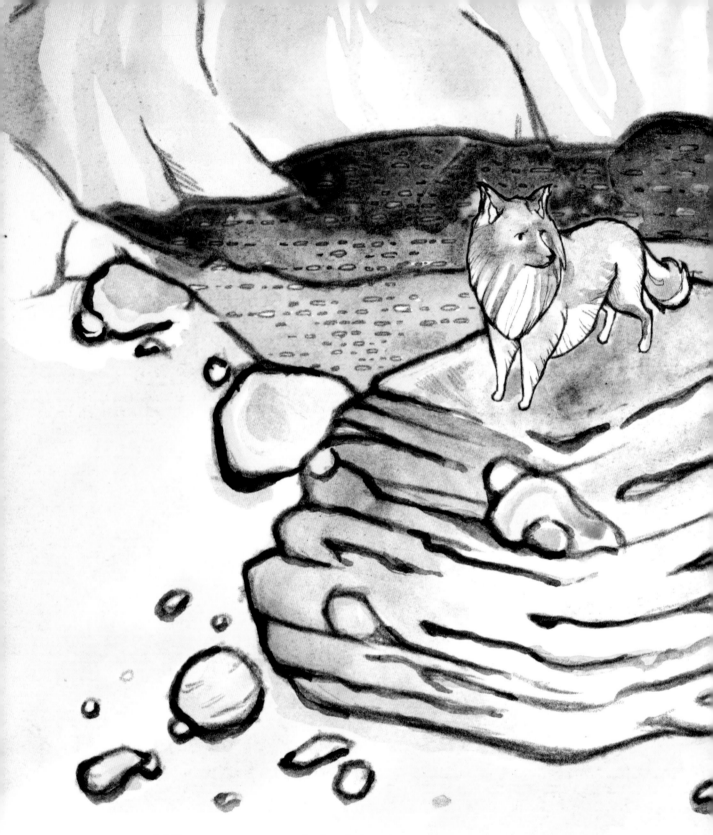

Winter came, and the lake fell silent and still.
Without the black wolf, the wide glacier felt empty.

Rangers seized a pelt of thick, black fur streaked with gray and scarred at the muzzle, taken by illegal hunters when the smell of fall hung in the air. The hunters were arrested and punished. But that didn't bring Romeo back.

One cold, clear day, Romeo's friends gathered at the edge of the ice-studded lake. Shawna sat next to the rock where Romeo used to lie in the sun, watching and waiting. She hugged Buddy's neck as grown-ups shared stories of the wolf they'd come to love.

Then the crowd fell silent. Shawna climbed onto Romeo's rock. She pressed a button on a portable music player. From the recording, a long, low howl pierced the air, a howl everyone remembered—the howl of the black wolf of the glacier.

Author's Note

Romeo was a real wolf who lived near Juneau's Mendenhall Glacier. Though no one knows for certain, it's believed that trappers killed most of his pack. His mother was likely hit by a car when he was little more than a year old.

Wolves are social animals. With no other wolves in the area, Romeo made friends with the dogs that lived and played near the glacier. Because of his affectionate nature, people began calling him Romeo. Shawna and Buddy are imagined, but their interactions with the wolf are typical.

Worried he might hurt a pet or a person, local rangers tried to scare the wolf off. A group called Friends of Romeo insisted he be allowed to stay, so instead of moving him the rangers posted signs reminding visitors that wolves are wild and should be respected.

In that spirit, Romeo lived for years near the glacier, leaving only occasionally to broaden his hunting range. Every winter, his friends waited for his return. But one year he never came back. Though it was hoped he'd found a mate or a pack to keep him company, the discovery of a black wolf pelt taken by poachers proved otherwise.

In November of 2010, Romeo's friends gathered at Mendenhall Lake to pay tribute to the wolf. They concluded the service by playing a recording of Romeo's howls. Though it ends sadly, Romeo's story reminds us of the dignity of wild creatures and the respect they deserve.

For more about this special animal, including photos, read *A Wolf Called Romeo: An Alaska Tale of Love and Loss* by Nick Jans. Thanks to the *Juneau Empire* for their permission to replicate one of their many articles on Romeo.